THE AUTHOR

HEYWARD C. SANDERS

Have previously published his first nonfiction story Equal Rights My Eye, then afterward he published the fiction story Creator, Creation and Betrayal, this story is a revise copy of the first Creator, Creation and Betrayal.

CREATOR, CREATION AND BETRAYAL

HEYWARD C. SANDERS

iUniverse, Inc.
New York Bloomington

iUniverse books may be ordered through booksellers or by contacting:

iUniverse
1663 Liberty Drive
Bloomington, IN 47403
www.iuniverse.com
1-800-Authors (1-800-288-4677)

ISBN: 978-1-4502-5392-5 (sc)
ISBN: 978-1-4502-5394-9 (ebook)

Printed in the United States of America

iUniverse rev. date: 08/31/2010

TABLE OF CONTENTS

A Note From The Author

Let me take the time to explain to you my reasons for writing this fiction story. We all have some understanding about the forces of nature which created a right way to do things, but through time the understanding was lost in man's perception of what is right, and through mistakes that were made. Instead of correcting these mistakes, they adjusted to them, and then came wrong to the land. After that, religions came to bring a better harmony and prosperity to all mankind, in order for them to understand how our Creator made us to be.

But there were some men's that could not follow the Creator's of Life ways. Then they decided to create their own path of what was to be life for them. I hope that this fiction story you are about to read will be a mind-opening experience, and will help the young people of the world find their positive energy in order to leave the world a better place in the future for others. Like they say, the thought is the cause of it all, and nothing happens by chance of accident.

Thanks, for you time and may peace and prosperity be with you.

—Heyward C. Sanders

INTRODUCTION

Have you ever thought about where the saying came from that people always use: "What goes around always comes around"? It sounds like the boomerang concept, doesn't it? Did the people of the world understand what that meant, or was it just a saying that we use in our everyday conversation? Or did the phrase come from a group of Tyrants and Dictators who understood that concept? Who were these Tyrants and Dictators? Did they try to confuse and trick the masses into waiting for something that will never happen without help from themselves?

Imagine that this was the case, and in the beginning of time, life was set up something like this. The Creator of the universe created all kinds of creations to balance the universe. All of these creations were created with different responsibilities to keep the universe in balance. The Creator's creations were born with positive energy, and they moved around the universe like kids on a playground. The positive energies did not have boundaries because they were already programmed, and the positive energy only knew how to do one thing. One of the positive energies was designed to do multiple things. Then one day that positive energy recognized how powerful they were. They wanted to see how far they could go in exploring the power they had, which created curiosity. Then came selfishness, then came scheming, and the twist went something like this.

We all were shopping in the store of life for the thing that gives us balance and understanding with the universe. One aisle says "retirement," and the other aisle says "life." In the retirement aisle is just retirement, because the Creator made retirement to be the end after the term of life, for our spirits to go back to that from which we came. The aisle marked "life" had in it love, health, righteousness, truth, justice, giving, fairness, honesty, prosperity, loyalty, good, harmony, strength, peace, respect for families, marriage to be between a man and a woman, and man and woman to live the way they were created to be. The "life" aisle's products had to be restocked every day. Their products were so good that they were selling out fast; they had to put the products on backorder.

The manager for the "retirement" aisle section did not like the role it had been given by the Creator. Once the Creator left to explore the universe for a moment, a member of the Creator's board saw the opportunity to take the chance to talk with the manager of the retirement aisle, and they saw the opportunity to make their move. The member of the board knew that the time was right, because who was left in charge? They had been waiting for this move for a long time; this was the member of the board they knew they could most easily trick. They brought to the member that the Creator left in charge the fact that it was not fair that the retirement aisle was not being shopped. See, the member in charge was not programmed to understand why the Creator designed the retirement aisle that way, but one of the members on the board, who was confining the member who was left in charge, knew — and the manager of the retirement aisle also knew.

When they spoke with the member left in charge, they said to the member that they were left in charge to make decisions for the Creator, and that the member and the manger of the retirement aisle felt that it was not fair for the retirement aisle to not be shopped on. The manager said, "I have a lot of good and fair ideals that can help both aisles."

The board member and the manager knew that the time was right to make the move, because the Creator of Life had left the board member called Fairness to run everything while the Creator was out. See, the board member who was trying to take over knew that Fairness was programmed to do what he thought was fair. So the board member made a suggestion to Fairness. Fairness was so caught up in being fair that the board member tricked Fairness into thinking that it was all right to make a decision without the Creator. It wasn't too hard for them to get Fairness to go their way, because the member knew more about Fairness and the things that Fairness was programmed to do. It wasn't too hard for them to get the approval for what they wanted to make changes in. The the managers had the OK to do whatever they wanted to do, as long as it was fair.

The manager automatically closed the life aisle and recalled all of the life products back as defected products. But some of the products knew something was wrong, and did not return because they did not know who was recalling them. Those who did not come back were natural things, like truth, strength, justice, righteousness, health, prosperity, harmony, loyalty, and honesty. And the tricky part of it was the manager's strategy was to move the life products to the retirement aisle, and organize each section from the life aisle to line up behind each new section the manager created for the retirement aisle. At first the retirement aisle only had retirement on it, because those other things did not exist.

The manager put these sections together so that the customers would not know what they were getting. Putting bad in front of good, hate in front of love, wrong in front of a fake right that the manager created, lies in front of fake truths that the manager created, taking in front of giving, trickery in front of fairness, violence in front of peace, disease in front of a fake health that the manager created, poison mind in front of a good mind, betrayal in front of a fake loyalty that the manager created, deception in front of a fake honesty that the manager created, weakness in front of a fake strength that the manager created, destruction in front of a fake harmony that the manager created, greed in front of a fake prosperity that the manager created, perverts in front of family, freaks in front of marriage, gays in front of man and woman the way they were made to be.

The manager was so smart that when the customers came in to shop, they all got fooled. They were buying everything on the retirement aisle so fast that the managers had to reorder the items in advance. The manager and one of the board members knew exactly what was going to take place if that happened. They knew that the world would change and that all living things would lose their lifespan or it would be shortened. Disease and poison came to the world. Then the plants started rotting fast, hate became the order of the day, and then came lies and deception.

The universe was taking on a new cycle of a transformation that it was not programmed to do. But what was so strange about who was orchestrating everything in the retirement aisle was that the manager, who was created by one of the members on the board, was named Satan. One of the members on the board programmed Satan to play any part and be the master at it. They say Satan never sleeps. One of the members of the Creator's board used to sneak Satan around *some of the members, so Satan could be around some of the board members that the Creator created, to trick the ones that Satan found easy to convince that Satan was one of the members of the board.*

Long before Satan met with Fairness, Satan had been coming through from time to time when the Creator was out exploring the universe. This was the first time that Fairness met with Satan because Satan knew to stay away from all the board members who were hard to convince. Satan plotted and tricked in an attempt to change the thinking of some members of the Creator's board, convincing them to go with Satan's thinking about trying to take over. They knew that Satan was tricky and smart, and could talk about any subject and master it.

You must remember that the world is the classroom, nature is the tool, and experience is the teacher, so don't you be the fool!

CHAPTER ONE

Wolves In Sheep's Clothes: Lawyers, Judges, Congressmen, And Senators

Satan and all the allies called for a world meeting on how to rule the world. At the roundtable everybody there complained to Satan. They wanted to know what kind of protection that they would get when they betrayed the Creator of Life with Satan, and when the Creator found out of what they did against life's ways. Satan tried to explain to the members that everything was under control. But they knew how Satan worked, that at any time they might get tricked by Satan, making it look like they thought of the idea to betray the Creator.

Satan said to them, "Everything I'm about to show you, I want you to go out in the world without me and see it for yourself, and report back to me of what you have seen." Then Satan said, "These are the things that you will witness; you will see that wrong controls right. That lie's control truth and taking control of giving. Trickery controls fairness. These are just a few of the things that you will see if you line up with me."

Satan continued. "And when you come back from touring the world, remember the problems you saw that need to be tended to, so we can talk about them at our next meeting when you all get back. When we are together we can find a solution before it gets out of hand. This will be one of our greatest moves we will ever do together. I know once you witness the things that we are talking about in the world today, you will never fear the Creator again."

So the allies left the meeting and went out to see the world to investigate the things that Satan told them to look out for. Satan knew when they returned that their fears would turn into fake strength and that they would be all the way on board and that Satan would be their new leader to rule the world.

Upon their return, the allies came back to the meeting, moving around Satan, blowing energy and saying, "Hail Satan, the new ruler of the world!"

Then Satan spoke. Today is a new beginning. We have to incorporate groups to stay alert at all times, because there is a small percentage from the life aisle scattered around that are not together, moving from place to place, trying to bring a rebellion against us, those who are loyal to the life movement. It is your job to train the area that you control to be on the lookout for groups that are congregating, and stop them from trying to bring rebellion against our movement." Then Satan said, "For all groups that oppose the movement, your team will have to make them believe that they hate our movement too. Our followers will have to infiltrate those groups and learn everything that they are talking about, and try to work their way to the top as one of the leaders. Then they will assign your allies to organize and pick their own groups to lead them, to help use destroy their movement."

Then Satan spoke again. "I've been waiting for this day to happen. I created a group of servants to use that have been waiting for this day. Later in our movement they will be introduced to the members of the committee. But right now we have to get everybody organized for their part that they need to play. You have to convince your area that everything is all right and that their sickness is good, and that hate is healthy, and for them to practice it all the time in their everyday life. See, we have to always let wrong lead and when wrong has to be corrected, we have to correct wrong with wrong and that will be our right. We cannot ever let them know what right is. Right cannot ever exist in our world." Then Satan said, "There is no such thing as right in our world, we only know wrong and more wrong, and if someone comes to your group with a different energy than what you feel, and you know that energy will be your enemy, and then it will be easy for me to introduce my new creation to the world."

Satan continued, "My new creation will confuse the communities so badly by twisting everything around. Then they will meet our new creation, early death, and that there will be no such thing as right, but all wrong. They will inflate everything so that the truth will no longer exist in the world."

Then one of the members of the committee said to Satan: "How will that be done?"

Satan stated to the members, "If we play our part real well in confusing the world, then time will permit them to be conditioned to our laws, and it will become the way of life for them. Then they won't know anything else, but that the laws of the land will give them two choices —and both of the choices will be in our favor. It's our job to trick them into thinking that one lifestyle is better than the other lifestyle. But we know that this is not true, and we are not the only ones who know what we are doing against the world. They will be trying to inform the world of what we are doing, and will try to start a resistance to rebel against what we are doing. They are part of the life aisle's members that did not come back when I recalled them. We have to stop them from trying to enlightening the world."

3

A member of the committee said to Satan, "How will we know who they are?"

Satan stated to the members, "Like I told you earlier, it is easy to recognize the enemy because they will be representing the natural things; truth and strength and righteousness, health, justice, prosperity, honesty, and harmony. Those are the only groups I know that did not return when I recalled them back from the life aisle when I tried to trick them to come back. Those are the groups whose energy is not like ours, who will try to enlighten the communities we are going to control. But when I introduce my new creation to our team, it will not matter what they try to do to stop us or how they think. Because my new creation will twist everything around so badly that the communities will not know what to believe. That's when you all should come in and makes the communities feel comfortable with your theory."

Then a member of the committee said to Satan, "We have been hearing so much about this new creation, when are you going to introduce it to us?"

Satan spoke to the committee, "You all are right, it's time for me to introduce my new creation. Let me take the time out to introduce our new members to the committee that has been programmed to work so hard on our behalf. Our first new member for you to meet is Congress, who will make the decisions for the communities that we control and will create laws that will start trouble with other countries. Congress will create the wars that we need to keep other communities in the world so confused that they will be happy just to have nothing. Then my creation, Military, will fight the wars that Congress created to conquer other lands, and police the communities that we already have control over. Then my creation, the Senate, will come to organize and represent the communities to bring negative things into their lives that Congress will pass for them. Then I have created the Judge, who will enforce the laws and bills that Congress will pass for our movement.

"But this creation will do everything that we need done. Let me introduce Lawyer to the committee. It will twist everything around so badly that you will not know what's right or wrong are, and will inflate everything so badly that the communities will turn into zombies and follow all the laws without questioning them."

Then the Lawyer spoke to the committee. "We have been programmed by Satan to protect all of you, all work from the oppositions, and to manipulate the communities to confuse them to think the way we want them to think. And we will take control of the situation at all times, and show the opposition that the ones who are working in our behalf they will not be able to control them. See, the world was designed by the Creator of Life and you all are supposed to function the way the Creator intended it to be, but the strange thing about it is that you all never stepped outside the box to challenge the Creator. We were programmed by our Creator, by Satan, the new leader of the world, to challenge nature. Today is that day, the day of the new movement. "Lawyer continued, "I learned how to trick the communities into questioning themselves about who they are. Just one minute, that's all we needed to put that thought in their minds. The thought is the cost of it all. I made a move and tricked the communities so they would think that everything that you are doing the Creator actually created it, in order for them to adapt to the forces. Just doing that alone made the communities questions themselves. Now all we have to do is keep everything going in the right direction. And we will see that male creation acts like female creation, and female creation acts like male creation. The wars played an important part in the change of this movement. See, by introducing fear to the world, *it makes things very easy for us to control. Fear is the tool that will open the path for negative thoughts and doubt, and once that negative thought is open, it's our job to never let that negative thought close up." Then the lawyer said to the committee, "The mind is what we want to control, and the easy way to do that, is to instill fear and doubt into their minds. That itself will make them so confused in their way of thinking."*

Lawyer kept on talking, but a member of the committee stopped Lawyer and said to Satan, "We the committees all are with you, but what part we play to help serve the movement?"

Satan said to the committee. "I have been waiting for someone in the meeting to say that. All of you need to play the important and most enjoyable part."

The members of the committee were excited to hear about the roles that they were going to play.

Satan said to the Sun, "I need you to make it so hot in some areas that nothing can grow, so the ground will crack because it's real dry. By us having control of their minds, we will program them to lie down and suffer. And Wind, I want you to move so fast that in some areas we will see everything has been blown away, so it will take some time for them to regroup. And Rain, I want you to make it rain in some areas so that the water will rise up high and flood everything out so that they must keep starting over. And Cold, I need you to make it so cold in some areas that ice will grow on the land and nothing else. Then their minds will not be on anything but trying to find a way to survive."

All the members of the committee that were asked to play a part said to Satan, one by one, that they would be able to do their part for the movement.

Satan said to the members, "Then we will be able to control the earth in the way we want things to be done. Now that we have everybody on board, it's time to go to work."

In the meeting everybody cheered Satan, saying again and again, "Hail Satan, the new ruler of the world!"

Then Satan said, "We have to work from sunup to sundown. We can never be caught sleeping until we throw the world off course; then we will have groups programmed to watch our creation for us." Satan stated, "Wherever you see peace, it's your job to make trouble, and where there is trouble, it's your job to make them feel that trouble is good. We have to push the world into being so selfish, that they will not be able to trust each other in anything they do. Then we are making progress in building a New World order for our master."

The committee was shocked at what they heard, because they thought that Satan was the Creator of sin, but when Satan told them about a master that Satan had to report to, they all were very curious as to who could that be.

One member of the committee said, "We all thought that you were the master of the world."

And Satan said, "I am, but do you know that each one of us was created by a Creator? Some of you were created by the Creator of Life, but you all did not like your role in that life. I was also created by a member that was created by the Creator of Life who did not like the role that life gave them. My Creator sits on the throne with the Creator of Life, and that's why I am able to get these things done so easily. My Creator is just as powerful as the Creator of Life. See, the Creator of Life gave my Creator the biggest and the most responsible obligation of all the members of the Creator board."

The members were so curious that they started thinking in secret with themselves to themselves about who that could be.

Then Satan said to the committee, "Are there any more questions that you want to ask?"

One member said, "When will we see the Creator?"

Satan said, "In due time, but not before we have to put all our minds and time on the movement, and not waste time worrying about the Great One." Then Satan said to the committee, "As of today, we have to stay alert, because the movement has already started. Today we are going to see a lot of resistance that is against us. See, when we play with nature, the forces were fighting hard not to change, and through that fight there was resistance that was born; lightning and thunder were created from the resistance, and their forces are quick and fast. Their power created some of the aggressive resistance in the world. Now, you know where the resistance came from. It's our job to stomp them out before they get too big and recruit a force that is so strong that it will be real hard for us to win. We are going to see a lot of resistance that is supposed to be against us, but when we trick nature, that itself will make some resistance get weaker. So, we have to target the resistance that we know is not strong and confuse them as to what part that they are supposed to play."

A member of the committee said to Satan, "How will we recognize them?"

Satan said, "Let me explain all the signs to you, so that when we enter the future it will not be hard for you to recognize them. Through the wars that were created by us, slavery came. When we conquer communities and their spirits have been broken, and the majority of them are so weak that they will believe anything and get with anything. Half of them will be with us. Half of the other half will be undecided, and the other half of the half will be with those who resist us.

"The ones that are undecided we should push to join the resisters, because in the future they will play an important part in our movement. The things I am about to show you will be the weak spirits that we need to exist with the resisters. You will see stones that glitter and rocks that come out of caves or mountains that they will be worshiping and will kill for. You will see some male creations acting like female creations and female creations acting like male creations, and you will see the male and female creations having a lot of orgies and a lot of rape in their communities. And from that you will see distrust in the communities. You will see that spirits are so caught up in themselves that they became so selfish and from selfishness there will be greed. You will see lies, and from lies will come betrayal. You will see hate, and from hate you will see killing. You will see dislike for no reason, and that will bring on loneliness. These are some of the things that you have to look out for. Those are the ones we need to stay on the side of the resistance for now."

Then a committee member spoke and said to Satan. "Why is it that we want them to be with the resisters?"

Satan spoke to the committee and said, "In the future these weak ones will be there leaders and will be running their movements, so you should understand now why I want them to stay with the resisters." Then Satan said, "Do you remember when I said to the committee that they will be playing an important part in our movement? You must not forget those ways. You must remember everything I told you about their weaknesses, because when you enter the future they will have new names, but will still have the same ways. You must recognize those behaviors, and not names. And it's our job to spot weak ones in the resistance movement and put more pressure on *them, to make the resisters think that they are strong. Just remember that in the resistant groups you will see three types of resisters. One group will be aggressive; one group will be aggressive but will stay with their congregation; and the other group will be passive, and will let you walk all over them."* Then Satan said, *"Just remember, we want the passive ones to lead the resistant groups, because we already have control over them. The other two we have to destroy by finding a way to discredit their aggressive ways in trying to bring us down. We have to trick the passive groups into making them think that the aggressive groups are working against the movement, and that they are with the enemy who is trying to destroy the movement by being so aggressive for the cause, without thinking of the damages being done to the movement."*

Then a member of the committee said, *"Could that be done without making them notice who we are?"*

Satan said, *"In the future, words are going to be our secret weapon. Using your words properly will trick the community into getting anybody you want, and they will work with you to destroy them. It's your job to know our allies when they do not know themselves. Their weakness will play a big part in identifying them, but it's your job to make them think that they are strong."*

Then the committee said, *"Hail Satan! Hail Satan, the new leader of the New World!"*

Satan said to the committee, *"I have to make a run to see some other creations I created to play a different part to help us build the movement, but before I leave you must know that we are going to be more powerful than life ever imagined we could become. And may the forces of hell be with us on our journey to control the New World."*

The world has taken a wild turn. Over a period of three thousand years things started changing, and the things that Satan implemented in the past started affecting the world. Everything started to function backwards. "Killing" became a new, likeable word, and then the word "death" came. Everything was working just like Satan said to the members of the committee, and they all felt more confident in doing their part in controlling the world.

Chapter Two

Among The Dead Is Religion

Satan came to have a meeting with some of the nonbelievers who did not have a say in what they wanted to be part of, which was created by the Creator of Life to represent life that was forced upon them. They all sneaked out to meet with Satan to see what was going on.

Satan said to the nonbelievers, "Are you ready to make this move?"

A nonbeliever said, "We've been waiting for you to arrive for a while, because we cannot stay with this program any longer but we do not know what to do. So Satan, it's time for you to tell us when you are ready to make your move. We want to have fun and enjoy ourselves all the time, and do not want to have to worry about what we are doing wrong and how we are doing it."

Satan stated to the nonbelievers, "The time is now for everybody to be in place, where I position them to be. Now it's up to you all to be able to play your part that I assigned you." Satan said, "I need to know what you saw and whether you were able to infiltrate their movement."

One of the nonbelievers spoke, "We learned from you, Satan, how to make the resisters think that we are against you and ready for anything that you will try and bring to us, and they elected us to hold high positions in the movement that was created."

Satan spoke and said, "What are they?"

One of the nonbelievers said to Satan, "They created clergies to spread religions. But we created doubt amongst the members to confuse them into seeing things our way."

Another nonbeliever said to Satan, "Now when they speak to the community they will have the community confused about what they are saying."

Satan asked the nonbelievers to explain how they got that to work. One of the nonbelievers said, "We used what you told us to do — twist the truth and make the lie sound like the truth, and the truth a lie. It wasn't so hard to do with them being so confused. But the tricky part of it was that we made the lie look better than the truth."

A nonbeliever said to Satan, "Don't worry, Master, we've been programmed by the things you've been teaching us. We can only serve you well, and nothing is going to get past us without being destroyed"

Then said Death to all living things, and "Hail to Satan the new master of the earth!"

Satan spoke, "The time will come when some of my creations will join you."

One nonbeliever said, "In what way will they identify themselves when we come upon them?"

Satan said, "When that time comes, you will know who they are, because they will think and will have ways just like yours." Satan then said, "See the resisters cannot fool you. They are not programmed to trick us, so you will always know who they are and when they are in your presence."

Then a nonbeliever said to Satan, "Are you saying that the resisters can only do one thing?"

Satan said, "Yes. I am saying that it is easy to spot them because all they know is the truth. They cannot come any other way to trick you that they are one of us, not them. They cannot lie to you that they are one of us; they cannot be freaks or perverts or homosexuals that will also be one of us. So it's not hard to recognize a resister when they are in your presence. They will always be the ones against everything you say because they will be speaking the truth."

One of the nonbelievers asked Satan, "How else can we serve you?"

Satan said, "Go out to the four corners of the earth and spread sickness and lies and wars through religion. Make every religion hate the other religion, and make them think that they are supposed to conquer the other, and make them think that they are submitting to their Creator." Then Satan said, "Do every wrong thing that can be thought of and make them think that their Creator of Life doesn't want them to do anything but pray for them, and to complete their full life cycle and to enjoy themselves while waiting to retire. Make them so weak that we can walk all over them, and make them so weak that they will see what we are doing and turn the other way, and won't acknowledge what they see because they think that it's the right thing to do. Make them think that the only thing the Creator want them to say is that they will pray to the Creator of Life to take care of them on Judgment Day. We have to make them think that it's all right to forgive us on every wrong thing that we do to them, because they think that we do not know any better. Then you will be helping us create group of nonresistance who will not be in our way when we conquer the world. You have to get into every religion all over the world and weaken their spirit and replace it with false hope. You have to make them think that their Creator doesn't want them to do anything but good deeds, and that the Creator of

Life will reward them with the Afterlife by giving them streets paved in gold and pearly gates, or giving some a thousand virgins for their good deeds."

Satan said to the nonbelievers that we determine what good is supposed to mean, that is because I took care of life, and also those they had to determine what "fairness" was supposed to mean because I also took care of fairness and replaced it with fakes.

Then Satan said, "The ball is in our court. Just do what you do, but always let them think that they only possess within themselves no more than five senses, because we tricked them into thinking that they only have five of them."

The nonbeliever said to Satan, "What are they?"

Satan stated; "See, hear, touch, smell, and taste. Those are the only ones that we want them to know about." Then Satan said, "The world was designed so that all living things are in tune with each other, and that every creation needs the same thing that the earth needs to sustain itself; the plants, the air, the water, the sun, the moon, and more." Satan said, "The universe is your spirit. It holds everything together in order for things to be in harmony with each other. And it's our job to trick them into thinking those things they possess that are part of how the Creator of Life created for them, that they do not need those things to exist in the world, and that there no such thing as a Creator of Life that they created everything on earth."

Then Satan continued, "I'm working on a new creation for them to use as a substitute so they will never need those things. But right now I need you all to take care of your part; then I can work on the other parts of the plan. See, you all have to find the ones that are in the movement with the Creator of Life, because they are going to try to stop our movement. They will not have the names that you all are familiar with. I heard that some are calling the Creator by the names of Jehovah, God, Allah, Buddha, and a lot of other names all over the world, depending on the language they speak in their country, and they are calling the resisters that got away prophets or messengers. When you see groups that are congregating, you might see one of the prophets or messengers."

Then one of the nonbelievers said, "What do you mean when you say they might be a profit or messenger?"

Satan said, "It might be one of our groups congregating trying to trick the communities to see our way of thinking. You have to join them and study their words and make the community love you like they love themselves, and then we can get into their souls. The good part is by the time they reach you; they will be confused because of my creation. They will have already broken their souls down so much that they will be weak, and anything you bring to them that looks all right they will jump on. All you have to do is get rid of the prophets and messengers and take their places." Then Satan said, "Now it's time for us to get together so we can make our own religion, and make the other religions respect our religion so much that our religion will be the decider of what's going on in the world. Then we have to enslave minds to work for our cause, and we will pay them with the promise that they will be the over seers of the new earth. Everything we do now will help us in the future in controlling what we can introduce to the world. We are planning and designing the way we want everybody to think, and their thoughts will create their actions. We need to introduce perverseness and homosexuality and freakiness into the religions, and let religions act like that they do not want those lifestyles in the religions." Then Satan said, "See, these lifestyles came from the past. Some of my creations created these lifestyles a while back through wars and greed and selfishness. Now we have some of our movement in high positions that care for those lifestyles that are part of the religious movement. So, all you have to do is stay in high positions in the religious movements, and when they try to rule against those lifestyles, you have to ask them to forgive the sinner, and convince them that only the Creator of Life can make that judgment. Because everybody in the religious world will have been programmed by us to commit at least one sin that they want to keep, and want the Creator of Life to forgive them for the sin that they commit. And if they can ask for forgiveness every time they commit that act, we want them to think that the Creator of Life forgave them, so they can keep on doing it over and over again until it becomes a way of life for them. See, we want to be able to tell the whole congregation to take the poison because the Creator of Life is waiting for them in the Creator's house of love and peace."

Satan continued, "And if we can make this happen now, then in the future they will look at it as a normal thing that is supposed to be."

Then one of the nonbelievers said to Satan, "I will enjoy this turning the world into a freak world."

Satan then said, "That lifestyle is part of our way that we are forcing on the world that is under our control; you must remember that we have to preach to the religious world that Satan rules the world and that the Creator of Life rules the universe. By the time we enter the future, everybody will be programmed into saying and believing that. Let me explain to you all the things you need to know. We cannot fight the resisters head-on — do not ever try to do that. You must remember that the only way we can win is by weakening them, and then our fight will be easy."

Then a nonbeliever said to Satan, "Why? Because we Master are not afraid of the resisters?"

Satan spoke to the non believers and reminded them that the resisters have positive energy and that control the power of action on their side, and that Satan and the nonbelievers were a negative substance they have on their side against the positive force to trick them in believing into creating a negative action. So, explain to me how you think that you can take the resisters without any energy that you possess?" Satan said to the nonbelievers. "Let me explain to you how the forces of the universe go. A negative and a negative is a negative, because they do not possess any energy that can bring a force. That is why it's our job to trick the positive energy into doing things we need done."

A nonbeliever said to Satan, "How about germs, is that a positive force that we bring to the world?"

Satan told the nonbeliever, "That is a positive force, but it was not created from a negative force, it was created from two positives that came together that were not supposed to be together, or got older and started to rot, but that itself still does not have anything to do with negative force."

Then the nonbeliever was ready to say something else, but Satan stopped the nonbeliever from speaking. "Let me finish what I am talking about, and then you might have a better understanding of how things work." Satan then continued and said, "A positive and a negative is a positive because the positive has control over the negative, because the negative is not a threat to the positive. Only when the positive gets older or we find a way to weaken them earlier. See, the positive flows around the negative because there is no energy to challenge the positive force. Nothing gets in its way because we are not energy. But the positive and the positive is a negative."

Then a nonbeliever said to Satan, "How can that be?"

Satan spoke and said, "Two positive forces will react when they are together because the Creator of Life made them different, and they have energy do different things. When they cross each other's path, a reaction will take place, and sometimes that reaction will create a powerful force against the universe. See, the positive forces do not know the power that they *possess, and without this knowledge a lot of negative things happen. So now you should understand why we have to keep the positive energies against each other, because they will destroy the world for us. You must not forget these things we are talking about, because the day will come when you will need this knowledge. The only way we can win this war is by trickery and nothing else."*

Satan said to the nonbelievers that trickery would weaken their spirits, and then they could implement their ways into to their lives. "We must use their energy to build our world without them knowing what is taking place. We cannot fight the resisters because we cannot fight. Our place is to trick the resisters into fighting themselves — to bring confusion amongst them, and all we have to do is lying back and watch them destroy themselves and their world." Then Satan said to the nonbelievers, "If you can do that, then you will be doing your job for the movement. You have to make them think that the prophets and messengers are more important than the message, and as long as they think that they will put all their energy into worshiping the prophets and messengers, and not the message." Then Satan said to the nonbelievers, "See, the prophets and the messengers arrived in the world to represent the laws of the Creator of Life, they bring to the positive energies of how to work together in a harmonious way. But every thousand years or so we find a way to disrupt their way by pitting positive energies against each other so we can have our way with them. Then they turn on each other so badly that they forget about what we are doing to them, and they start hating each other in a nice way by saying what the Creator is going to do to them, and that they will pray for them. See, the worst thing that happens with them is every one of them wants to be the leader, and none of them wants to follow. See, they do not really want to follow the ways of the Creator of Life; they just want to talk about it and that's all they will do."

And Satan said, "That is what we want them to do, and then we will be able to implement our lifestyle into the world. Then selfishness will be the way of the world for all."

Then Satan said to the nonbelievers that he had to move on to see what the other creations were doing. Before Satan left, the nonbelievers said to Satan, "Do not worry about us, Master. Everything will be done on our end as you requested." Then they said, "Hail Satan! Hail Satan, the new ruler of the world!"

The world took another turn for two thousand years or more and everything that Satan said for the nonbelievers to do to create the future happened, and things were more confusing than ever before. The resisters were fighting a hard battle, trying to bring order back to the world, but the longer it took the harder it got. The negative force was building energy off the positive, and they were so strong that the negative force took over everything that got in its way. The New World was exploding with a lot of out-of-control energy, and the world came to be more violent than before, but was justified by doing it in a civil way.

CHAPTER THREE

Where Is The Living With The Dead?
Doctors And Pharmaceutical Drugs

Satan came to talk with the creation named Science that he had created. Everyone came to the meeting excited to tell their master of what devious things they had done to help Satan control the New World. When Satan appeared the members said, "Hail Master! Hail Master, the new ruler of the world!"

Then Satan spoke. "I come here to report to you the things that took place in the past, for you will know that everything is on track in creating the greatest movement that ever took place against the Creator of living things." Satan then said, "Wars have started, slavery is the order of the day, and killing is taking place and the earth smells like death." Then Satan said, "Perverseness and homosexuality and freakiness are the order of the day. We made the future come to us."

Then Satan asked the scientists if they had seen any of the prophets or messengers that were supporting life movement that were trying to stop their movement. Satan said to the scientists, "Now it's up to your movement to finish the final work that we need done."

Then one of the scientists said to Satan, "Welcome to the New World, Master of the earth." And then they started explaining the things that they created.

"First let me answer your question about the prophets or messengers that are with the life movement. They haven't been seen here. Your movement in the past might have already destroyed them. What we see is a lot of weakness in every group that is supposed to be with the Creator of Life. These groups we see are afraid of the truth. They love to talk about things that they know are not going to happen. Fantasy is the order of the day. That's how they make themselves feel good, by lies that they know are not true. They live off their desires and feelings. These groups have become replicas. What that means, Master, is groups without souls. All we have to do is let the groups think that we have something good to offer them, something better than the group that they are following, and they will serve you well. This is better than slavery. Controlling their minds is the greatest move you ever made, Master. You cannot tell the religious world from the pagan world. The religious world does the same things the pagan world does. They are eating the creatures the Creator made, and they pick over the ones that they will keep for pets. Sometimes they make me think that they are us, because they are doing everything we do — and more! These religious groups are so much like us, Master. The New World of religions is like you said it would be if everybody stayed on course in the past. Each religion hates the other so badly that when they are in the presence of one another, you can see their dislike for each other."

Then Satan spoke. "They are nothing like us because we have a purpose for what we do; they do the things that imitate us because we programmed them to act like that. You have to remember that we limited them to only five senses to control their way of thinking. Now they are so weak- the way we want them to be — that they will jump on any lifestyle presented to them."

One scientist said, "I see, especially the weaker ones that have been pushed around all their lives."

Satan said, "Those are the ones that we want, because when they have power over the communities they will abuse their power."

A scientist said, "Why is that?"

And Satan spoke, "Because every weak spirit wants to have the opportunity to be a strong energy one time in their life, and all the things that happen to them will make them a good candidate for what we need from them. They will beat the communities down and will do every illegal thing that you can think of just to have power that they are not used to. They will move around and try to weaken the strong energy, and will work with us to keep them down."

Then one scientist said, "It seems to me that it sounds like they are mad about something."

Satan said, "They are all for not being strong, and they will take it out on everything in their path."

Then the scientist started back, saying, "Your Congress and Senate have created new groups from the past that are called 'parties' for the communities, which they make laws that they set for the communities to obey. These parties are called the Republican Party and the Democratic Party, and are controlling everything in the New World. Every country has to confer with them before they make a decision against another country. And they fight amongst each other so badly that the groups had to separate themselves even amongst each other. One group is calling themselves the Right Wing Movement, and that's supposed to mean that they are with the Creator of Life, that all things stay in their natural order. And the other one *is calling them the Left Wing Movement. They are supposed to be for the artificial world that was created by you, Master. These groups are so weak that they do not know at any time what they are talking about. They are so confused about who they are and what they are supposed to be about, that the communities that are following them are lost. And the religious world followers are also confused about why their leaders want the congregations to stay like that; because that's the only way their leaders can stay the head of their congregations. The only thing they are doing is running their mouths, acting likes they are with the Creator of Life, and after everybody leaves you will see them do everything they tell the congregation not to do. The new word for them is 'hypocrite.'"*

Then Satan asked, "What are they doing to make these leaders that are called hypocrites?"

The scientist said to Satan, "They are freaking with some of their congregation, having homosexual acts with some of their congregation and doing perverted acts with some of the younger ones in their congregations. And they love the materialistic world that you created in the past, Master; they love jewelry and slick clothes."

Satan asked what jewelry was.

The scientist said, "The stones that you talked about in the past that they will kill for — called gold and diamonds and other names, but they all are put in the jewelry category. They still will kill for them and sell each other out. This jewelry thing is one of the most powerful things you created for them to worship, Master. And the other thing they will kill for is the female creations with those freaky desires that you created in the past, which created wars and dislike trying to please the female creation's needs. The female creations have the male creations doing everything and anything in trying to please them. The male creation is beat down so badly that they do not even have a say in what is happening. The future will destroy them, like you said, exactly the way it would happen. Their purpose in living is to worship the female creation and not the Creator of Life. They live only to leave all their strength in the female creation to serve their sexual desires, and they have nothing left in them to conquer anything that a male creation is supposed to do." The scientist said, "Everything you said earlier about what the future is going to be is happening, Master. Everything is on course with your plan to rule the earth."

Then a scientist said, "Master, they are so caught up in materialistic things that they do not know what right is anymore."

Then another scientist said to Satan, "Now, let me explain the things we have done that you programmed us for. We have been programmed so that every detail that was put in us we used to the best of our ability, and every obstacle that came our way we learned how to get around. In the New World all the obstacles that were in our way from the past are not here in the future. Master, your groups must have been taking care of them, or they went underground trying to regroup from the whopping you gave them. The only ones still here are natural things, but the things that we have created would stop them in playing an important part on earth."

Satan said to the scientists, "What is that?"

And one of the scientists said, "We've been experimenting on how to create a world of artificial things that we will have control of, and that everybody will buy our produce before they buy natural things."

Then Satan asked the scientists how far they had come with this experiment, and one of the scientists said, "We already created a way to preserve the food they eat which comes from nature."

Satan asked the scientists how that would that help them. One of the scientists said to Satan, "Master, the preservatives that are in the food are *artificial, and they will break their systems down in time. The good thing about it is that they will not know where the problem came from. We also learned how to turn their food into processed food, with all types of chemicals in it that will break the body down in time."*

Satan ask what the chemicals were, and one of the scientists responded, saying, "We invented some chemicals by putting different types of minerals together that do not belong together, which will produce a reaction. They won't even know what's going on with them. And the natural drug they are using to cure their problems when they are sick or in some kind of pain, we are making an artificial drug. By the time we enter the future, we will have control of the drug market — if you, Master, tell Congress and the Senate to work with us by outlawing the natural drugs as illegal. This will help us in two ways in controlling the masses. One, making the natural drugs illegal will make the masses only have but one choice, and that is to use the artificial drugs that will break their system down slowly; and two, we will be able to create more institutions to enslave them legally for using illegal drugs."

One of the scientists said, "If we don't stop them, Master, from using natural drugs, they will be able to grow their own drugs in their backyards, and the natural drugs will restore their cells in their bodies, not destroy them."

Another scientist said, "Master, there are a lot of things we need your creations Congress and Senate to do for us. We're going to revolutionize the world to the artificial world with the help of Congress and the Senate."

Then Satan said to the scientist, "That sounds good, but what is it that you want Congress and Senate to do?"

One of the scientists said, "We need the Senate to go out into the communities they represent and preach to them with some of their allies in those communities that the artificial move is the best thing that can happen in the future. And then have the Senate submit it to Congress to pass, and let Congress argue it for a while so that the communities will think that the members of Congress are looking out for their best interests."

Then the scientists said to Satan, "If you can get Congress to pass all the things that we create for the future, Master, you will see the final touch of the world you created for us to rule."

A scientist said, "The artificial world is a creation that will work on our behalf. It will destroy the way their communities think and make their bodies react real different from the way they are supposed to function. It will also create mood swings so that they will not understand what is happening to them."

They then said, "Master, nature is the last of the resisters. Let us take care of them, because we've been here creating the master plan of how to take the natural world out from controlling everything, and in the future you will see that the artificial world is king of the land. And we are going to have doctors that will prescribe to their patients more than one prescription of artificial drugs, and we will have pharmaceutical stores that will be housing all of the artificial drugs."

Then Satan spoke, "The time is here. We all are in place now and the future is around the corner. Now we have our religion in place to rule the other countries. Now it's time to make a country that we have full control over and will have the other countries follow ours as the leaders of the New World." Then Satan said, "We have to program everybody in our country, and I mean everybody, to think negatively, even when they think that they are positive. The only way we can do that is to control their minds by using signs and symbols in the world, and it will play a part in shaping their way of thinking." Satan then said, "First, when someone runs for office and is *doing the swearing in, we have to make everybody use the Right's energy on the bible and not the Left's."*

One of the scientists asked Satan, "Why must we do that?"

Satan said, "Because we can never close the Left's energy up. We have to let the Left's spirit be open to run free, and let the Right's energy die. Then we have to make everything so that it are being used from the Left, and then you will see a change in how they think."

Then Satan said, "We have to make right illegal and wrong legal in our country, then the world will be ours. In the New World we want the replicas to run our country for us because they cannot think, and we can use them to oppress others in the way we want things done. They will follow orders, so show that you have their reward for them."

And then a scientist said, "What is that?"

Satan said, "In our new country we have to make every bad thing good, and every weak thing strong, and then reward them with the power in controlling the land and they will serve you well. You have to make everybody love the materialistic things so much that our new country will be the leader of the materialistic world. And then we will have control over their minds in destroying them. First we will have to make them think that they cannot live without the materialistic things, and without them they do not want to live. And then we will have to make them steal and take from each other to possess the materialistic things, and also to kill for them and love doing it, because killing will give them great power over the others. And then we have to make them feel that it's all right to kill themselves when life is getting hard and they do not know what to do. That will be for the ones too weak to fight back, or for those who are just tired of living because they ran out of ideas for what to do. Then in the future we will have power over the ones that think they are right, but find out that their right is not supported by the communities. Rather, it is hated by the communities for enlightening them to the truth of something that they already knew about, but were too scared to do anything about it because they did not want to lose their benefits. And by the time we enter the future, that one will be so weak that they will kill themselves because nobody likes them, or will do something crazy against the communities or at work, and in their minds they will justify it as being the right thing to do."

Satan continued, "The day has come when we enter the new country. We all will be there, and that it will be our biggest meeting that we've ever had since the takeover. I'll see you all in the new country. "

Then the scientists said, "Hail Satan! Hail Satan, the new leader of the world! Death to all living things, and let the smell of death lead the new country."

The world had been taking a turn for hundreds of years, and the scientists had played a big part in the change. Things were shaping up exactly the way Satan planned. The members of the Creator's board were more confident in Satan's plan. And Satan's creations were proud of their master. Everything was on the course that Satan projected it would be. Satan would return to the Creator's house to report to the one that created him about the new information in controlling the world. Satan knew from the Creator who created him that there would still be some resistant forces out there because the resisters recruited a lot of people to fight with them, but Satan knew that the new country's energy would be extremely negative from the things they did in the past, and he hoped it would stomp out all positive energy that was against the negative force. Satan knew the resisters were strong and would never give up their fight for the Creator of Life, and that the battle had just begun. Satan entered the new country that was *created for them to rule the world from there. Satan came to America, the new country for the negative force.*

CHAPTER FOUR

The New Country America Short Lives, Out-Of-Control Sex, And Following The Path Of Destruction — Hollywood

Upon arrival, all of the movement members were there to welcome Satan to the New World. They wanted to do something special to welcome the new ruler of the world, so on that day the members of the movement rolled out the death smell that spread all through the world. A lot of things were dying and wars were creating killing and looting in the communities, raping and torturing, fires were burning, there were droughts in some places, and flooding and freezing in others. It was the best welcoming Satan ever had. Their forces moved all around Satan, saying, "Hail Satan! Hail Satan, the new master of the world!" Then they said, "Hail to the king! Welcome home to your new country!"

Then Satan spoke. "We all made it to the future and that in itself tells me that everybody stayed on course. I acknowledge all the members that are here. Those who did not come are the board members representing the ones that came to represent the Creator of Life's board members that could not come. This day is long-awaited, and stemmed from our determination of who controls our thinking of how the way we want to be programmed.

This is the biggest meeting that we ever had, and might be our last because now we are the world, and everybody will have to stay in their position after today."

Then a member said, "Master, it's true of what they say about you."

Satan said, "What is that?"

Then a member said, "They say you never sleep and are always planning the next move to stay on top of the life movement."

Then Satan said, "Thank you. I take that as a complement. This is how we must be at all times. You must not forget that we are not our workers, and that our ways are normal for us, but make our workers weak and lazy. Just imagine if we slip into their ways. We would no longer have the power over them, because we became like them, and that will set our movement all the way back to the beginning. But the good part about it is that will never happen, because we were programmed different than them. See, they were programmed so that they could be easily weakened and slip at any time, because those habits they cannot control; but the same habits are normal for us because it's our way of life."

Then Satan said, "Now, let's get down to business. I need to be updated on the way the new country is and how many of our sicknesses have arrived here. So, I will start at the beginning of the movement with the members of the Creator's board who are representing them." And then Satan said in a joking way, "Take all the time you need because we now have all the time in the world."

So the first one came up and said, "I am the heat that represents the sun. The sun brought dry land and drought and famine to the world."

Then Satan said, "Explain what you mean."

The heat said, "There is a shortage of food in some countries and the land is so dry that they cannot find water. The ground cracked because it *was so hot, and that they were fighting and killing just for water. The sun made it so hot that they were being burned, and all they wanted to do was to find some shade just to relax in. The sun made it so hot that the forests in many areas caught on fire, and every community around the forests caught on fire, too. The sun sends me to say that from the beginning to now, they have been loyal to the movement and will be there to the end."*

Then Satan said to the heat, "Go give the sun my loyalty, and tell him that we will still be calling on your powers every year when it is your time to come back around. The Creator of Life created you all to keep on doing the things to bring order in the world for our movement."

Then Satan said, "Let's hear from flood, which is representing rain."

"I come on behalf of rain to bring our report of the things we did for the movement. First, I have to say that there is only one king that runs this world, and that is Satan, our leader of darkness. I come to bear gifts for you, our king. We have brought rain for weeks nonstop, flooding some countries so bad that they are under water, and the only thing they can do to survive is try to float on a log so they will not drown. We bring death through diseases, germs, and infections and we pollute the water with a lot of toxic waste that kills all living things that live under water. We create so much litter that the fumes are unbearable to smell and we also created the smog so thick that it's hard for anybody to see. We make tides to push them out of some communities and have to run for higher ground and leave their worldly treasures behind under water. We bring high waves that rise over anything in the water and swallow it up and sink it to the bottom of the sea, and their worldly treasures are left there for thousands and thousands of years. Rain also wants you to know that we control seventy percent of the world, and that seventy percent is loyal to you, our King of Darkness, and

that we are on call at anytime that we are needed for the movement. I rest my case in representing rain."

Then Satan said to the flood, "Give the rain my loyalty, and tell him that we will be still calling on your powers every year when it's time to come back around, what the Creator of Life created you to keep on doing things to bring order in the world for our movement."

Then Satan said, "Let's hear from cool, which is representing cold."

"I come in behalf of cold. First, cold wants you to know that it has been an honor and a great pleasure to have been given the opportunity to ride with you through thousands and thousands of years in the sin of darkness, and it has given me nothing but pleasure to report the things we have done for the movement, my king. Cold wants you to know that we have taken a continent and have frozen it so that nothing can grow on the land but ice, and that it gets so cold on the land that it will freeze them to death. We make snow fall from mountains that comes down and destroys communities. We made it so hard to survive on the land that the Creator of Life's creations' life spans has been shortened to half of their normal cycle. We made it so hard that the only two things they do are hunt for food and to try to stay warm, and the only things that they can find to eat are the Creator's creations because nothing can grow on the land. In civilized communities, with the help of rain we freeze, everything that they need from us on the outside will to slow them down. Cold wants you to know, our King of Darkness, that we are loyal to only one power, and that is the King of Darkness."

Then Satan said to the cool, "Give the cold my loyalty and tell him that we will be still calling on your powers every year when it's time to come back around, what the Creator of Life created you to keep on doing things to bring order in the world for our movement."

Then Satan said, "Let's hear from breeze, which is representing wind."

"I come on behalf of all the wind families and we want to thank you, King of Darkness, for trusting us and giving us the opportunity to be part of this great movement. It gives my family nothing but great pleasure to have been able to travel thousands and thousands of years with you, and it will be an honor to ride the rest of the way for the movement. Wind wants you to know the things we have done for the movement. We have blown the air so fast that the Creator of Life's nature was thrown around and knocked down. Communities they built themselves were destroyed, and it takes them a lot of time to rebuild. We also took the air and blew it real fast— so fast that it got three times faster than the air we normally blew, which made nature fall on the communities. This one rose so high that it started speeding around in a circle and pulling up anything that was in its way— and I mean anything! It takes everything with it when it leaves and drops out what was lifted miles and miles away from the spot where it was taken from. We also assist flood with the big waves that rise so high, and assist cold with the snow that falls from the mountains, and to freeze nature's things to fall on communities, and to freeze the food that they grow to eat. Wind's family wants you to know, King of Darkness that for thousands and thousands of years we have been riding with you— that our loyalty is so strong that we look at you as part of our wind family."

Then Satan said to the breeze, "Give the wind my loyalty and tell him that we will be still calling on your powers every year when it's time to come back around, what the Creator of Life created you to keep on doing things to bring order in the world for our movement."

Then Satan said, "The Creator of Life's members play one of the important parts in our movement; they kept obstacles in the way for us, *and the most important things they have done were to keep a secret from the ones on the Creator of Life's members on the board who are not with us. And now it's time for us to hear from some of my creations. Let's start at the beginning of the movement, where I introduced Congress."*

Congress said, "Good day, and what a good day it is. Our king is here to enjoy the land we created for you. I remember a lesson the Creator of Darkness told us about how to fight the resisters, but we were so strong in manipulating energies we thought that nothing could stop us from getting to the top. Then one day we ignored all the things our king was telling us, and because of that we were set back in claiming our new country for the king to rule, and other countries from there.

"And upon our arrival there were communities of resisters that welcomed us, because we had the passive resisters went on land first, and they were welcomed by the native resisters. The passive resisters was so glad to see other resisters and to be welcomed to the new land, because at the old country the passive resisters were being knocked all around, and anything that they thought was theirs was always taken from them. So, they were excited to see the New World. We used them to make friends with the resisters and to tell them that we come in peace. By them being so passive, they wanted to believe that story. They had the native resisters so relaxed that it was not hard to make our move to take over. We started a move from the old country to bring all kinds of negative energy to the new country fast, and without screening the negative energy that we programmed, things got out of hand. The negative energies were so negative that they did not want to follow orders; they felt that nobody could speak for them any longer, and that they could do anything they wanted to do.

"They started rebelling against our movement and refused the things we did not want the native or the passive resisters to see. The native resisters

saw what was going on and started arming themselves to fight against us, but before the fight started we had already programmed some of the native resisters to see our way. By the things you told us, Master, we used the same tricks that were used on the passive natives, and got them to work with us. They showed us all of the things that the native resisters needed to survive and we poisoned them all. But before that they were so strong that they took over the country and had us running. That's when we sat down and went back to your plan, and things started to get back in order for the movement. And then the passive resisters came. They started making rebellion moves against the movement; some of them were spies for the aggressive resisters to let them know when the time was right to make their move on us. And by some of our movement exposing how we really acted, the passive resisters knew that they would not be able to trust us, so the battle began and the aggressive resisters were so strong that they ran us back to the old country. In your words, King of Darkness, a negative and a negative is a negative, but some of us infiltrated into their movement and started back all over again. So we apologize for taking too long in bringing you to your country to rule the world from here."

Then Satan said, *"I understand everything that you all had to do because the resisters learned how to trick you all through the weaker ones, and that I did not tell you how they can use the weaker resisters to do their work. See, the weaker resisters belong to everybody, any group that trying to get up, and they are going to use them first. So that's just the way for all groups to get in through the weaker resisters, and it has nothing to do with the things you all did wrong."* Then Satan said to Congress, *"Is there anything else that you would like to say?"*

Congress spoke and said, *"We'll let Senate finalize the things that went on in the new country, my king."*

Then Satan said to Senate, "It's time for you all to tell me what part you played for the movement."

Then Senate said, "Thanks, my king, I will start where Congress apologized for not taking the country earlier, then we ran into a strong resistance against the south and a war started. It was the south against the north. We were run out of the south and the north took over the whole country. But we still had some allies that were left in good positions in the south, and were told to go along with the resisters until we saw the opportunity to make our move again.

"See, king, all the three resisters that you talked about in the past that we thought were wiped out were here in the future — and stronger! The passive ones, we had them working for us in the country, but everyone was going to have at least one or two double traders that were only working for themselves. These resisters still functioned like they did in the past. One group was passive, and those we control; and the ones that stay with their congregations, they stay in rural areas and still live off the land. They want nothing to do with the modern world or society, and are real strict in their faith. And the aggressive resisters were the ones we had the biggest problem with. They were still going around the countryside, spreading the truth to anybody that wanted to hear them. So we got into the communities and started campaigning against them, telling the communities to watch out for groups that were going to try to trick you into thinking they come with the truth of what the Creator of Life wants them to be. Our biggest setback, King of Darkness, was those replicas. They do not follow any orders, and to be truthful they are in our way. They brought more setbacks to our movement than progress. Their loyalty is with no one because they cannot think. Any position that we put them in, they will mess everything up and set us back because they do not have a purpose in being part of the world.

They are just in everybody's way, both ours and the resisters. When we made them kings of darkness in the past, at first they played a good part in the things our movement needed them to do, but now the future is too advanced for them to follow. By them only knowing five senses, the future will eat them up. My King of Darkness, I rest at this time and pass it over to Lawyer to tell you the rest."

Then Lawyer started off by saying, "Good day, Great One, the King of Darkness, the master of the world, our guider and teacher, and May the smell of death reward you for many more thousands and thousands of years on earth. We had to figure out how to change the laws that resisters put on the books when they rose to power. These laws were carved in stone for the new country to follow, were set for the lifetime of the country. This is where we had the opportunity to use the replicas again. See, King, the replicas outnumber every group, so who controls them? Who controls their vote? And they've been with us for a while, and we still have power over them. So we used their numbers to make new laws and erase the old laws that were set in stone. See, the old laws still exist because they are set in stone, but the tricky part of it, is that the communities are run with so many replicas that they do not care about anything but enjoying themselves. So, we changed a lot of laws back to our way of life, and the Senate brought it up to Congress to pass , and Congress did what they always do — they let it sit while they argued, making the communities think that they were looking out for the best interests of the communities. See, the voice from the communities is more powerful than the laws that were set in stone. Then things started coming back around to our ways, how we wanted the country run, but the resisters were fighting the new laws that Congress put forth. But the judges that were with the movement enforced the new laws that Congress set.

"*Things started coming back around and the resisters were more determined to try and change the laws back, so we came up with a way to make the resisters appear as criminals, and the communities went with the laws. We started calling them outlaws and the name 'resister' faded away through the years and our movement was called 'regulators'— those that control the communities. Then things came all the way back into order and the death started flowing again for us. The communities went back to being in controlled by us. Then we got the laws passed to have our lifestyles lead the country to the freaky ways and perverted ways and the gay's ways. Bills were passed, and everything was ruled by those laws, and the country went back on track in the order that we wanted it to be. Then we created big companies to run the new businesses that we had brought to the new country. We incorporated the companies to control the masses' needs and their wants. The future was shaping up and the more the future came, the less we had to worry about the resisters. The replicas grew strong in numbers, so our votes got strong. We imported a lot of new replicas from the old countries we control because time was running out for the replicas that were here, and we were replacing them as they burned out.*

"*Then we incorporated a company that would help our companies get their products sold and control the masses. We named the new company the 'media.' It would give only the news we wanted the communities to know. And it would describe all the products that we wanted to go out to the communities, and tell them the good things they could do for them. The news media also keeps us up-to-date on where the problems are, and they talk about the crimes in the areas, and that in itself lets us know how our work is moving through the communities. The communities got programmed into believing everything the news media said. Their way of thinking was controlled by the news media and our products moved fast. That was a wise idea when we created the news media to inform the communities. It paid off well for our movement in keeping order the way we want within the communities. Our companies started doing well because all of our information was getting out to the communities, and the communities are now shopping in every company that we have.*

"See, the best things that happened to our movement were thousands and thousands of years in the past. During wars we enslaved countries and made some of the slaves fight with us for their freedom; then after they became free and powerful, they bought slaves and brought them to this country, so all the slaves were trying to serve their masters for their freedom. Then during the wars we found out how the slaves could better serve us. That was when we came up with the ones who accepted our way of life and would ride with us to be free. Those times in the past set the trend for today's movement in controlling the replicas to follow our laws. They have been conditioned to love their sickness and the materialistic things that come with it. And by controlling their minds, we've made them think that they only have five senses inside themselves to guide them. So the business world was growing fast and the new replicas came in on time to take the place of the old replicas, because they got so weak from living our lifestyle that a lot of them were catching all kinds of diseases. And we still rewarded them with more of the new materialistic things they loved, and opened a lot of sexual clubs for them so they could enjoy themselves more. So everything got back in control for us. I rest my case and pass it over to our great scientists to finish it up."

"Good day, Master of Darkness, the King of the New World. It gives us nothing but pleasure to see you on your throne in the new country. It took time, but the things we learned during the transition made it worthwhile for the time that we spent working on it. It taught us how to get to know

more about the ways of the resisters and how they think, and which of the replicas' groups will better serve us in our needs. By picking the right replicas to serve us, we placed them with the resisters in the aggressive movement to help them fight us. As time passed, the replicas became the leaders, because we knew that they were strong fighters, but had no thinking ability and were programmed to think that we were the smartest power in the world. That itself made our power grow so much that the resisters started fading out and the new country was open for our laws to take control.

"Congress passed the laws for our prescription drugs, and we opened stores to house them, and through the replicas, these are now the biggest population in the country. Our drugs were selling so fast that we had to submit our orders in advance to the companies that manufacture the drugs so we could better accommodate their needs. And ninety percent of the foods in our stores are processed foods with all kinds of artificial preservatives in them, and they are shopping in our stores so often that we leave some stores open all day. This is our country, King of Darkness. We are controlling everything now and they are eating out of our hands for more of the sickness that we control.

"Congress passed the laws that natural drugs were illegal and the new prisons started building up so fast to house those who were violating the laws. And Congress passed one of our greatest drugs, one we prescribe for the females who do not want to have babies. We made a pill that can stop them from having babies so that they can have all the sexual relations they want — so they can have all the fun. Congress passed the laws for everybody to get wild and free, and sex was so wild and crazy, and then some females forgot to take their pills to prevent them from having babies.

"These prescription drugs will play one of the greatest roles for us to rule the world. See, these drugs the weaker resisters and replicas are taking

— when the drugs leave their bodies they are being discharged back into the water systems, and that same water will be restrained and cleaned to be used all over again. Then the process repeats itself over and over again. The best things about this process is that the water is being processed over and over, thousands and thousands of times, with different chemicals, and our team of scientists tells them that the water is safe for anything they need to use it for. We put a strong chemical in the water to purify it so we can run the same system back through their communities. That chemical they use is only for cleaning the bacteria, which are germs in the water system, but is not strong enough to destroy all the prescription drugs, or any of the other chemicals that are there. And that will help to destroy their system so badly that their minds and bodies are programmed by the chemicals in the water to shut down over time. They will think that something else is happening with their bodies because of something they just took earlier. It is also making the females act like males and the males act like females. The water system is playing a great part in controlling the thinking of the weaker resisters and the replicas.

"The good thing about our teaching, which we learned from you, Master of Darkness, was the five-sense concept. The weaker resisters and the replicas were programmed to use only their five senses. That itself played an important part in using them to do our work for us. We send them to our schools for twelve years, and some stay up to sixteen years. We have some who have gone all the way to twenty-two years of education, and they do not even know what we are doing to them. All the schooling does is to teach them how to run our companies and nothing else, because they do not know or understand their bodies and the other senses the Creator of Life created in them. They are so content in building our world, and that will destroy them. And Master of Darkness, when you said one day they will be running

things for us, and we will be able to do other things to keep the movement moving that is exactly what they are doing for us now. We can spend our time on other things and they will watch and run our stores just as if we were running it ourselves. The future is just like the way you said it would be, Master of Darkness, if we stay on course.

"Then Congress passed a law for our doctors to go inside the female womb and suck the life out of them. Everything got back on course and our way was flourishing. We invented a pill that Congress passed to make males turn into females and a pill for females to turn into males. Congress was passing everything and anything we thought of, and the communities went along with it because we had groups out there telling the communities that nobody should be able to tell them what they can or cannot do with their lives, and the plot thickened. They got so conditioned to wrong that they would argue for a wrong to be right, and would kill you for that wrong, thinking that wrong is the way it is supposed to be. The country grew back the way we wanted it to be, and the smell of death got stronger and stronger. As you would put it, my King of Darkness, a negative and a negative is a negative, and a positive and a positive is a negative. We learned that saying well, and incorporated it into our way of thinking. Once we started understanding that philosophy, it was not hard to keep a positive and a negative apart, and we never did bring them together to function with each other.

"Everything you told us, King of Darkness, we learned how to master in order for the future to go our ways. We knew that weakness was our way of life and the resisters' way of life was strength, and nothing we did to try to weaken them would work. The only way to stop them is to kill them. That's why we made the country go into to our way of life as the aggressive resisters, no longer exercising the laws that our Congress passed, causing a *lot of them to be killed or go to prison for the rest of their lives. The resisters that stayed amongst themselves lived in secluded areas in rural communities, and every time they came to our communities they'd be laughed at for living in the past. By us programming them from the past, it was not hard for the weaker resisters and the replicas that lived in our communities to live with that hatred, for the strong energies to believe that we programmed them to think — that they worked hard to make it happen and that the weak would be strong and the strong would be weak. They loved that saying so much that they put those words on the walls of their houses. Our control of the way they think helped us to make the truth become false, and that falsehood become the truth.*

"We created a fake world in the past for everybody to follow in the new country. King of Darkness, we created a lifestyle just for you so you could enjoy your country. We made a Hollywood where everybody is faking and acting, and we made them to be the leaders of the communities where everybody worships them and watches them and wants to be like them. And we made them target their children real young to be part of our world, and the children grew up famous and were rewarded with so much wealth that every child wanted to be like them, and the parents did not care that we were introducing them to our lifestyles because the wealth kept them silent. We did have our way with their children. All of our perverted, freaky, and gay ways, lies, and hate went into them to introduce it to the country. And if the communities wanted the things that they had, they had to start acting like the leaders they looked up to, and the country went all the way into our lifestyle. The communities' children started talking back to their parents, acting out in all the wrong ways we like them to, and they took over the country for us and implemented our ways all through the land. And the years made the children become adults, and they started making

love to their children and our ways ruled the land. And the big companies incorporated them into their companies as CEOs, managers, supervisors, and other things. The more power we gave them the more they worked hard to destroy anything that would try to stop them from enjoying their lives of power.

"My Creator of Darkness, we are working on an experiment where, in the future, those natural things will be a thing of the past and the country will be one hundred percent artificial. We are experimenting on genes and how to make them turn into sperm so that two females who are in love with each other can take their genes and turn them into sperm, and inject it into one of them to carry their child. And two males who are in love with each other can take their sperm and inject it in a female to carry their child so the child will have both of the genes of the child's parents. We're experimenting now on some of the Creator of Life's creations now, and things look good for the future. Then we can get Congress to pass a law that it will be illegal for a male creation and a female creation to be together. Then the prison system will destroy everything that was in our way to control the country, the other countries will follow us in everything we do because they recognize that we are the country leading the world to better things for the future. We now are working on replacing all replicas and weak resisters with robots that are programmed by us to do everything for us, and the good part of it is that they do not get sick or lazy. They follow orders right without us worrying about them working with groups against us. And the replicas and weak resisters will still have their quality of life by giving them monthly incomes that can take care of their bills and the lifestyles they love. I rest my case, Great One of Darkness, and it's a pleasure to serve you and help bring the New World here for you to be king over."

Satan spoke, and said, "It gives me great pleasure to know that I chose a smart team that worked together for the dark world, and made everything work out in our favor to rule the world. I knew that things were going to come your way that would try to stop you from making our world exist, but you all fought for darkness. That in itself shows me the Creator of Life's creation was not as smart as we thought they would be. Their strength was great, but their intelligence was weak. Just because they were not able to control the power that was given to them, they made decisions that set them back and put us ahead. The world is ours from the thousands and thousands of years we traveled across the world. The smell of death went to the four corners of our world. Now all we have to do is not to get cocky, to keep on ignoring the bad things, and imprison them for doing the right things, and the country will stay ours."

The world took another turn for about a hundred years, and Satan retired from traveling all over, and stayed in the new country that was built for the King of Darkness. Satan's creation took the place of traveling around the world, checking on the poisons they planted in communities that they did not rule, hoping that the future would develop and grow their diseases in those countries for Satan to rule.

CHAPTER FIVE

Man And Woman The Way They Were Made To Be By The Creator

One of Satan's loyal creations traveled to a land where the country was so strange that everybody was living in peace and harmony with each other. Satan's creation could not understand what was going on because they had planted a lot of negative seeds in that country hundreds and hundreds of years ago, and during their travels from time to time, they witnessed the poison growing in that country. Satan's creation recognized that things were not right, and started investigating what had happened to change the course they had set into motion. One afternoon Satan's creation followed the community into a meeting after work. Satan's creation was surprised at what was being discussed at the meeting. It was all types of positive energy and an energy that Satan's creation did not understand. The positive energy opened by saying, "Bless the Creator of Life and all who follow His words," and said, "The day is a special day for us all, it is time for us to travel the four corners of the world to represent our Creator's movement and take back the world for our Father." Then they said, "Yes, I said Father. Our love for the Father and Mother that created us in to this life, that we proudly carry their name and genes, that we will stand to represent them if someone or something says or does anything against them. Our Creator who created us — we should hold ourselves up to honor the protector of life a hundred times higher than our parents. And our parents should be telling us to honor the Creator higher than them, and say, 'I bear witness that there is only one great force in the world and I am proud to be the speaker, the protector, and the representation of that force.'"

Then the speaker said, "In the beginning, thousands and thousands and thousands and thousands of years ago, the world was one and everybody was in harmony with each other. Then a selfish energy emerged and recognized the things that it could do. That selfish energy created trickery and from that came lies, and from lies came hate. This selfish energy wanted to be bigger than the Creator of Life and the only thing they could think of was to destroy all of life's products. This selfish energy went about tricking people that were easy to trick with these products, and won their trust making them think that they were doing a great service to life's products. See, these life products were not used to lies and trickery, so it was easy for them to be tricked and lied to. Then came wrong, and the world took a shift into the Dark Age and nothing was safe anymore. Life products started retiring earlier than their time on earth, and diseases and poisons took over the land. From wrong, a creature was born. The creature's name was Satan, the ruler of darkness.

"This Satan learned how to manipulate positive energy into doing wrong things, and over the years, this allowed wrong to become right. See, one thing wrong knew that the other energies did not know was that wrong was a mistake, and if we corrected that mistake there would be no such thing as wrong. So wrong had to make that mistake thrive for

thousands and thousands and thousands and thousands of years in order for it to become recognized as a power. Then the power of wrong took over the land by confusing life's products so badly that no one could trust each other anymore. Fear took over the land, lies followed, and hate was the order of the day. Then came wars, and from these wars came control, and from control came slavery. And then came weakness, and from weakness was created perversion and freakiness and gay ways. The world was so out of control that the universe started reacting in the opposite way, not in the order that it was supposed to. Everything was thrown off course, and a new meaning was on earth. Now it's our job to bring the communities out of the darkness and back into the light. See, our biggest problem will be the ones who think they are preaching the Word of the Light, because they have been manipulated for so long that they think the dark is the light. They are the ones we will have to fight first, because they are misrepresenting the Word of Righteousness in all the wrong ways.

"First we have to realize that they will be our biggest fight, because we will bring a separation amongst them, because so many of them are caught up with materialistic things that they will destroy the Word before they give up their selfish treasures that they acquired by lying. They will report to the King of Darkness to let him know what we are doing and will work against us. They are so sick that they will try to stop us from bringing the world back into harmony. The only way to beat them is with their own laws, which the resisters built for all countries to follow. First is the religious world. We have to come down on any religion that says they are following the prophets' ways, but are lying to the communities. We have to sue them for everything they have. Taking their worth from them will stop their power and enhance ours. We have to hire inspectors to sit in some of their meetings and learn what they are talking about, and watch what they are doing for

the communities. We have to fight fire with fire and hire and train them to look out for the littlest things, because where there is a little problem, a bigger one is hidden around the corner.

"*See, the religious world was taken from us through Satan, the King of Darkness, by infiltrating into our ways by putting members of their movement in high positions in the religious world. Their job was to make all the religions hate each other and fight to destroy each other, and now the future has them killing each other and working together with the perverts and freaks and gays against each other. We have to stop worrying about the sinner, because they let us see who they are. That is in sin, but our big problems are the ones who are not letting us see who they are — those who hold high positions in our movement who are hypocrites. They are traitors to the life movement and should be punished by taking everything that they acquired from our movement, and thrown out on their faces for the entire world to see. Our job is not to preach to the misguided energies. No, that will take too long. We have to get our lawyer and file every violation that Satan did against the order of right. We have to file all violations on the new laws that took over the old laws that were carved in stone, and remove them, and we have to put natural things back and remove the artificial things.*

"*See, the biggest trick that Satan pulled on all countries was to put the energies against each other. By putting positive energy with positive and putting negative energy with negative energy, Satan knew that nothing good could come out of it. But he did stay away from putting positive and negative together. Why was that? Satan is and always will be the master of manipulation. See; let me explain to you about our energies. The soul of the world is based on all energies. That's what keeps everything balanced. Satan was smart and found a way to offset the universe, to throw everything off balance, by playing with the energies. See, Satan could not do this alone.*

The prophets teach us that a member of the Creator of Life's board created Satan and programmed Satan to be the opposite of right. By doing that, Satan created wrong — but the tricky part of it is that wrong is not real! It is only a thought that was created in your mind through trickery, and they acted on that trick by putting the same two forces together that caused a reaction against the universe.

"Let me explain to you the way our Creator of Life created us to be, and the good benefits of a positive and a negative joining together. Satan programmed the world for thousands and thousands of years, making the countries think that the negative is bad. If that were so, the positive would have fought against the negative and a bad reaction would have taken place and would have destroyed them both. The secret is in nature. Satan's creator knew that the negative was a positive at one time, but in time we're all going to be a negative. Our negative energies all around us help the flow of our progress today. Positive energy is like a kid on the playground, and negative energy is like the elder watching the kid on the playground. See, the positive energy is young and the negative energy is old. They work well together because the young energy is wild and crazy and it can make a lot of mistakes were it not for the negative energy, which guides the positive energy to stay balanced. See, the negative energy was the teacher of life's experiences. When they were a positive energy, they would learn from the positive energy how to flow with the order of nature. By Satan putting two positive together, it created a wild reaction because they are like two kids without supervision, and this created a force of violence. And by putting two negatives together, it made everything slow down because the elders' energy is not there anymore, so it was easy for them to lose their balance when the positive energy turned on them. Both energies were tricked to stay apart from each other for thousands and thousands of years — so much so

that they became conditioned to those ways. Then Satan sucked the energy out of them and killed their spirits, but left the bodies and turned them into replicas; that is, a robot that is programmed to do nothing but follow orders. Then you have some weaker energy is still fighting, trying to keep their spirits, but being programmed when they were young, it made things hard for them to understand the truth. They are confused about which way they are supposed to go. They do not know what is right or wrong, so it's hard for them to believe anything you bring to them.

"It's our job to get the lawyers that are among us to target the laws of nature and show us the way things should be to bring harmony back to the world. Then the two energies will see how they are supposed to work together to bring about harmony. Then we have to get our lawyers to target the communities all over the world to police their own communities and teach them how to protect their children by forcing Congress to pass a the bill to give back money to each comunity to hire or fire their own protection for their communities. See, we should have two kinds of protection; one for the communities that we will hire and fire when they are wrong, and one for the cities. There should be one for cities to protect the business districts where commercial businesses and industry lie. We also need to give back money to the communities so they can to hire and fire their own teachers. See, controlling our communities will help them keep out all the wrong lifestyles that might destroy their communities, which is the way Satan wants it. We have to teach them how to pick their Congress and Senate every election, and to make sure that they come from the good communities, and not put into to power Satan's helpers who are trying to trick the communities. We have to hold Congress responsible for making nature's drugs illegal, and locking up communities for using them for medical use. We have to show

how artificial drugs attack the organs in the body and break it down in time, destroying organs, which cause death.

"Our lawyers have to sue Congress for making the Creator's natural things illegal and programming the communities to like their sicknesses by taking artificial drugs, which are destroying their bodies. See, we were taught that the purpose of intellectual schools was and always will be the programming they were designed to perpetuate, tricking the world into thinking that prescription drugs are better than nature's drugs. First they had to trick the energies into thinking that they only had five senses, and programmed them to believe that lie that for thousands and thousands and thousands of years. See, the Creator of Life gave us so many senses that I am discovering more as my cycle changes and transforms me every ten years. I recognize seven of them all the time, but the others come when we need them for emergences to protect us. The seven are sight, hearing, taste, touch, smell, thought, and to create our thoughts from the other sixth sense. See, the emergency system that is built inside us is the one we were programmed not to know, so that the intellectual can have power over the world and push prescription drugs onto us. This makes them think that artificial drugs have more benefits and can cure them better then natural drugs — but it fails to tell them that drugs are not the cure. They only hold things together for the body target the problem, and then attack it. And the best drug for that would be a drug that worked with the body — nature's drugs that our Creator of Life made for us. These are natural drugs that we can grow ourselves. But they chose to make it illegal so the people will not be able to cure themselves. And it would also weaken the intellectual position over the world.

"Our prophets teach us that the Creator of Life is first, then communities, then family. It has nothing about the teaching of the pleasures for perverted,

freaky, and gay sex ways. We were taught that those were Satan's creations and to stay away from them if we wanted to keep a good community. Those lifestyles steal your spirit and soul away from you, and throw you off balance with the universe. Now, I ask you: Were the prophets right? Look at the communities that live with those lifestyles and see the sickness that is rampant among those communities. If it was a good lifestyle, we would not be here now talking about finding a way to save them from themselves. Our prophets Nature, Justice, Strength, Truth, and Harmony were created from the Creator of Life to come to earth and bring harmony to the Creator's creatures on earth. And each one was created to play a different part for the Creator of Life. Nature was created to bring nourishment to the land for all living things; Justice was created to make sure the laws of the land would not change. Strength was created so we could stand strong to our convictions for what is real. Truth was created so we could tell the true story about our Creator of Life, and Harmony was created to bring harmony amongst all of the Creator's creatures for peace and prosperity. There were more creations by the Creator of Life, but they were tricked by Satan, and were destroyed by the forces of their own energy pulling away from the truth.

"When we are balanced, the whole universe will be balanced, and the things that nature made will start to function again in the order that they are supposed to be in. We cannot spend all of our time trying to save weak spirits and broken souls, because the more you force the truth on them, the more they will run to the King of Darkness. They have been conditioned from the day they were born to love their sicknesses, and will fight us if we try to take it away from them. The only thing we can do is make a better world for their children, and reprogram them from childhood in order to bring them back in the order of to the way life is supposed to be. The weak spirits and souls will infiltrate back into the congregations with the

hypocritical leaders, and work together to destroy everything the truth has to offer us. They will water the truth down so much that they will make you think that the real truth is a hard thing to follow, and that the real truth was only for the prophets and messengers, and not for the Creator of Life's creatures. See, the materialistic world stole them from us, and we might not be able to get them back. It's like the saying about the rotten apple in the basket and what it will do in time to the others if it stays there. So, it's time to leave the dead with the dead and save the young. And if there are any livings amongst the dead, they will pick themselves up and follow us. We have to stop trying to drag them where they do not want to go.

"We have to teach them that they cannot let the King of Darkness fool them by telling them that they have to stay with their flock that the Creator of Life created. The Creator of Life made all creatures, but Satan tricked them and lowered their energies to hang with Satan. Our Creator of Life wants us to grow with energies that are like yours, no matter what kind of creation it is. You cannot join a group that your energy is not supposed to be with. Some groups will try to imprison your energy and force you to go where you do not belong. Our energy was created by the Creator of Life and Satan does not have this energy. Satan is lurking around and setting traps for our weaker energies in order to steal their spirits and souls, and to make it part of Satan's way of life. Energy is in all living things that our Creator created, and we are supposed to feel the energy around us to know what type of energy it is. No one is supposed to tell us what we know is wrong to follow, because they feel that it is the right thing to do as long as it does not hurt you. That energy that they are following is with Satan, and he knows how to use the right words to persuade them.

"We have to go to the four corners of the world and find the resisters that stood their ground and resisted the temptations that Satan offered them, and

work with them to bring all the tribes back together to bring harmony to the land. We have to teach them how to put their differences aside, and for them all to come together for the one common purpose of restoring the land that Satan destroyed. Our job is to teach and to learn the things that they know about Satan's ways, as well as the tricks that we do not know about. See, by us not being victims of Satan's temptations, and living in a country that is anti-Satan, we have to listen first to what they have to say about the King of Darkness, and how the evil forces took over their country, and sucked the life out of the weaker spirits' souls, and forced them to destroy they way of life the Creator made for us. Then we have to teach them and show them the way back to restoring their land, and how to save the young spirits and souls in order to bring them back to the Creator's way of life. We have to let them feel our spirit so they will know that we come with the truth and that the Creator of Life loves them for standing against the evil forces that were pushed on their country. See, they have been tricked so often that they do not know the truth when it comes before them, so we have to take our time to understand them and work with them so they can feel our spirit. Then they will know that we are the ones who come to free them from the bondages of the King of Darkness.

"We have to go to the four corners of the earth and bring order back by seeing to their needs. Where there is a country that is too hot and the community is suffering from heat and drought, we have to bring to those countries solar power systems to bring cooling systems to their houses, and use the solar energy to pump water to their villages. See, on earth there is more water than land, so there is no reason why water cannot reach little countries or villages. Wherever the water is, the energy from the solar system will pump it to them. And in cold countries that have a lot of wind, we have to make windmill energy to warm their homes, and we have to bring

water to the land so they can grow food and make an income by selling their food to other countries. We have to train them to teach their kids how to keep their systems going, so the knowledge will not be lost in the future. It's our job to show them that using nature's tools to take care of them will be all that they need. The world is so messed up that they do not know how to put order back, even if they wanted to. It's our job to show them how to do what's right and restore the world back to the order in which it is supposed to be. We have to teach them how to fight Satan with our way, and not Satan's way, by showing them that our voice is more powerful than any violence, which is the King of Darkness's way. We have to go to the four corners of the world, to small and undeveloped countries, and train their lawyers in how to put documentation together of what super powerful First-World countries did to their countries. We should bring them to the world court for criminal acts against the natural way of how things should be. And we should teach them that violence is not the way — its Satan way, and it should not be their first choice or last choice, it should only be a forced choice and nothing else.

"And if that forced choice comes upon us, may all the energies in every country pull together with the Creator of Life to bring about a new struggle that no wrong force can ever control. See, we have to make every country look at itself and target their own demons, and stop criticizing other countries for the things they have at home. It's easy for them to take up arms up with the King of Darkness; that is, to go against any country that would not follow the King of Darkness's ways, which they do not follow themselves. We have to challenge the ones who say they walked through the valley of darkness with no fear, because they might be the darkness — because they should be able to show you the path to the light. And if they cannot do that, then they are the darkness.

"*See, you cannot say you have seen it and have gone through it all, but cannot guide your congregation to the light. If they are saying to be humble and peaceful living in the belly of the house of darkness, then you know what side they are on. The followers of the Creator of Life would never accept the ways of darkness to have control over them, and would resist to the Creator of Life's call for them to retire. If anyone in a congregation came and told you to submit to Satan's ways because their congregation still has the right to practice the Word, run as fast as you can.*

"*Our prophets also teaches us that the earth we live on has mood swings too, and the cycle comes every two to five hundred years. Where there is water, it will turn into land, and where there is land it will turn into water. These are some things that scientists are not going to tell you, that some cold areas will get warm and some hot areas will get cool. The earth is just taking its cycle change like everything else does. See, we do not know the reason this happens, but I can say at no time have we been without air to breathe. Things have to be recycled and cleaned somehow. See, the benefits that our Creator of Life has for us we do not understand. These things will happen without us worrying about them. The process takes place without us knowing that it is happening. Some might say, 'Why the Creator of Life would put our communities under water?', and I can say, 'Why we build everywhere that we're doing, that we not supposed to?' See, we cannot blame our Creator for our selfishness in doing things without considering the consequences of our actions. Greed brought this about, and complacency made us stop thinking about the things that we do to ourselves. Then at the end of the day we blame the Creator of Life for the big mistakes we did to ourselves.*"

Satan's loyal creation had heard enough, and left to report the things he witnessed to Satan. Satan's creation came upon the Master and started explaining the things he witnessed in this country that they thought they controlled. Satan was so angry that it was the first time that the Master of Darkness's creations saw him react with all kinds of illusion that they did not understand.

Then Satan said, "Kill them! Kill them all! They are trying to destroy our work that we've created for thousands and thousands of years!"

Then one of Satan's creations said, "Master, if we react in that way, the weaker resisters and the replicas will know who we really are and will try to break away from us."

Satan calmed down and said, "We have to find a way to stop them from getting to the other countries."

Then one of the Creator of Life's board members, who had betrayed the Creator, asked Satan about the meeting that they were having for the return of the Creator of Life, and asked if Satan was going to be there. Satan said to the representative that they would be there. Satan could not tell them that he was never to be seen by the Creator of Life. They did not know that Satan had never seen or been in the presence of the Creator of Life. One of the members of the board always brought Satan around when the Creator of Life was out touring the universe. All the betrayed energies were scared because they did not know how much information the Creator of Life knew, and who would be the first to betray the other.

CHAPTER SIX

The Creator Returns From Exploring The Universe

At the meeting everybody gathered around, looking to see who was there. The Creator of Life spoke and said, "I have traveled all around the universe and have witnessed a lot of things that are taking place with the planets."

All the betrayers were so scared when they heard what the Creator said.

Then the Creator said that everybody would have a turn to speak of what they saw in the universe. The betrayers were thinking that something was wrong. They were looking around for Satan, or trying to figure out who is Satan's master was — and where he was — because they knew that Satan would come in disguise.

The Creator said, "Let's start with you, Fairness, since you had the power to take care of the kingdom that was left for you to run." Fairness said, "Welcome home, Master. I did everything like I thought that you would do, and things are all right. At first there was a problem that was brought to my attention, but it was taken care of, and things went back to the way they were. Everything has been quiet since."

The Creator said, "What was the problem that you had to take care of?"

Fairness said, "The retirement aisle had a problem of not being able to be shopped on, so I let the manager change the aisle so everything could be fair with each aisle."

All of the betrayers were shock at what they were hearing, because they thought Fairness was one of the candidates for the master who created Satan.

Then the Creator said, "Who is the manager and why did you feel the need to do that? And what was the emergency that caused you to take that matter up without waiting for me to return?"

Fairness said, "Satan is the manager of the retirement aisle, whom you Created to run it, Master."

Then the Creator said to Fairness, "Is there a manager on the life aisle that I created?"

Fairness said, "No, Master."

Then the Creator said, "Why do you think that I need someone to manage an aisle that does not have any purpose but one thing, and that is to retire at the end of everybody's cycle?"

Then the Creator stated again to Fairness, "Does the life aisle have a manager to take care of it?"

Fairness said, "No, Master."

The Creator said, "So, explain to me, why did you think that something I created to perform a specific function would need you to make a decision without waiting for me?"

Fairness now knew that they did a wrong thing, and said to the Creator, "I see, Master, that I made a mistake in the decision that I made."

Then Creator still said to Fairness, "Who is Satan and where did he come from? The Creator said; because I never created such a name to be amongst us."

Fairness was shocked at the things the Creator of Life was saying. Fairness said, "Master, I was introduced to Satan as being one of your creations by the Devil."

All the betrayers finally knew now who the master was that created Satan, and they were waiting to see what the Devil was going to say.

Then the Creator of Life asked the Devil, "What do they have to say?"

The Devil spoke, and said, "Master, I do not know what Fairness is talking about. I've been here doing the work you told me to do, and he's not a manager on my aisle." Then the Devil said, "I've seen what Fairness has been was doing, but I thought that you gave him the OK to do that. That's why I did not say anything to Fairness, because all I do is follow orders, Master, and you did not instruct me to say anything to Fairness about what they were doing."

Fairness was so shocked by what he was hearing that Fairness said to the Devil, "That's not fair, what you are saying. See, Fairness did not know how to express what was wrong but one way, and that was the way they were programmed."

The betrayers heard what the Devil said, and got scared because when their time came to speak they were so confused that they did not know what to say.

The Creator of Life heard everything that was being said and spoke to Fairness, asking, "Is it there anything else that you want to say?"

Fairness said, "No, Master, I said everything that I wanted to say."

See, the Creator of Life already spotted what was going on, but played it out, and said, "Who wants to be next?"

Everybody was quiet.

Then the Creator said, "I do not have to hear from the Devil, they have already spoken."

All the betrayers were afraid to say anything because they did not want the Creator of Life to catch them in a lie.

The Creator said, "Who is this Satan that is going around creating problems with the kingdom? Has anybody else witnessed this Satan?" Then the Creator said, "Let's start with you, Sun."

Sun was scared, but knew that the Creator of Life was onto something, and said, "Yes Master, I had some contact with Satan."

And the Creator said, "What was that?"

The Sun told the Creator that Satan showed them how to use their powers. The other betrayers were shocked that Sun was giving them up— and now they knew that they had to come clean.

Then the Creator said, "What do you mean 'them'? And how did you all meet?"

Then Sun said, "Satan was here in the kingdom when we all met him."

Then the Creator asked, "How did Satan get in the kingdom?"

The Sun said that they did not know, so the Creator said, "When you say that they don't know are you speaking for the others too?"

The Sun said, "Yes, Master, I am. We all thought that Satan was a member of the board."

Then the Creator said, "Was Satan in any of our meetings?"

And the Sun said, "No, Master."

Then the Creator said, "So, how could you all think that?" Everybody got quiet and nobody said anything for a while. Then the Creator of Life spoke. "There's no need to hear from the rest of the board because I already know what's going on and who played a part in helping Satan in everything that Satan did to the kingdom, and I guess that this Satan showed the rest of the members what the Sun was talking about — all your all powers."

Everybody was still quiet. They all were so afraid to say anything.

Then the Creator of Life went back to Fairness and said, "Tell me, what was Satan supposed to have done to the aisles?"

Fairness spoke and said, "I gave Satan the OK to change the aisles and make them one, and then everybody who was shopping on the life aisle started shopping at the retirement aisle because the life aisle was closed."

And the Creator said, "How did Satan get the shoppers who shopped in the life aisle to shop in the retirement aisle?"

Fairness said, "Satan took the life aisle products, the ones that were returned, back and lined them up with a new creation that Satan created, and the ones that did not return Satan made new creation in their image."

Then the Creator said, "You mean fakes?"

Then Fairness said, "Yes, Master, fakes as you will put it." Then the Creator said, "So, what happened to the real ones?" Fairness stated, "We do not know, but I think that they are still out there because they refuse to come back when Satan calls them back."

Then the Creator said, "Now, after you have heard everything do you blame them for not coming back?"

And Fairness said, "No, Master, I admire them for seeing something that I did not see."

Then the Creator of Life said to Fairness, "I forgive you because you were not programmed for the lies and tricks that were played on you from one of the members of the board." Then the Creator said, "This must have been something that they were trying to do for a while, but had to wait for the right member of the board to make their move. But let me explain to you all that the things that were done. There is no such thing is a Satan, because I did not create him, and if this Satan tricked you all to go against the kingdom, or if the one who created this Satan put him in a position to talk with you all, and you all went along with this Satan, I have to consider that this was something that you wanted to do all the time. The thought is the cause of it all, and you all had to have that thought in order for someone to persuade you to do something against the kingdom."

Then the Creator said, "Like I said before, Satan is not real, so the only thing Satan can be is an illusion that tricked you all to react and use your own powers to do Satan work." Then the Creator said, "Can anybody tell me what powers Satan had that you saw, or powers that this Satan used to trick you all to use your powers to do his work?"

Everybody grew quiet again for a while.

The Creator said, "I thought so." Then the Creator said, "I am not going to blame the Master who created this Satan, because the act was in you all to be tricked by Satan's illusion. That itself showed me how much you all wanted to go outside of the things that you were programmed to do. But let me say this to you. You did not do anything that you were not doing first. You perhaps didn't know what the thing was you were doing because you were not programmed to know. And this Satan came along and tricked you to think that you had done something new." Then the Creator said, "So, you and this Satan can try to put the blame on each other, but you only can blame yourselves because you all have the power — not Satan or the Master — to control your destiny, and you all chose to be with the illusion rather than the truth. My world is still the same and my loyal creations are still the same, so what is going on in your world? I am not programmed to see those things because they do not exist in my world."

Then the Creator of Life dismissed the meeting, and went back to sit on the throne to run the kingdom and to let the betrayers try to figure out what the Creator of Life had in store for them. Little did the betrayers know that the Creator of Life did not worry about what had taken place, because it did not affect the true believers' movement of all living thing to rule and protect each other.

My Closing Statement

I remember one time when a female coworker was correcting me about how I answer the phone in my office. She said that I was not answering my phone in a professional manner. We had some words, and then I realized what she was saying. I apologized for not being more professional. Then I explained to her why some males ignore the things that a lot of females say. It is because they lost their way from nature. Then I explained to her about our purpose on earth and the different roles we play to keep the universe balanced — and those they were not equal roles. I explained to her about that old saying about how one bad apple can destroy all the apples in the basket. Then I told her we were made two ways to serve the Creator of Life, and they are not equal. I said one, you are like the soil that is on the ground and your purpose is to protect the seed and nourish it for the entire lifecycle of that seed; and I am that seed, and by you nourishing me, I grow to become a great tree to produce good apples. But if you refuse to do your part, I will be weakened because you ignored your duties that nature gave you. Then the cycle of life changes for us all, and we do not know where we belong anymore.

If you take that approach against nature, you choose to side with wrong. Believe me, sister, when I say this man did not make up what I am saying.

Just study nature and you will see it for yourself. The Creator set these laws and we have to follow them. Every creature has an important part to play to keep everything balanced. We all are a whole when we work together and a half when we are apart. Man played an important role in destroying the balance by falling in love with his desires and not caring about the consequences that would follow.

When I spoke about energies that we should line up and find a way to be with the energies similar to yours, now I understand the relationship between pets and their owners, I remember my grandmother when she had two little dogs. Those dogs followed her all around the house and their energy was very much in peace and harmony with my grandmother's. The dogs acted like they were my grandmother's children. It was so strange to me because I thought that was so funny, being young and not understanding the relationship between owner and pet. I remember on weekends when I visited her that she was always a lady who did everything on time and about the same time. One day we were sitting down for dinner, and she made the two dogs their dinner in separate bowls, and she called them in to eat. They came running in and went to the two bowls without fighting over which one they wanted, and I was so surprised that they did not touch their food until my grandmother said grace. I look back at a lot of things and now I understand the relationship between owner and pet. Maybe that's why I talked about energies that are alike. Then we can also go to how people love their flowers, how and you might see some of them talk to the flowers. I watch how they treat the flowers and take care of every leaf, checking to make sure that everything is all right with them, and would argue with anybody if you tried to destroy them.

I remember a time when I was living in this high-rise building. I was on the elevator with a person who lived there too. He must have been watching me for a while, because he asked me what faith I was with at that time. He said that he was with the Buddha faith. I told him that I followed the Creator of all living things and not man's ways, because each language has a different understanding of how they are supposed to better serve our Creator of Life, and that nature is our path to understanding and how to stay grounded. Then man created different parties with a twist of how to better serve their needs and not the people's, and the people started following them more and lost their understanding of what the right way was.

Then we also can see the misguided energies who want to be something other than them and are always making bad decisions, trying to be greater than they are. These misguided energies do not want to wait for their opportunity to come to them, they do not have patience for anything; instead, they sneak around and try to knock you off your square. They want overnight what someone worked for years to get. The energies I spoke of are possessed with a bad force that is controlling their decisions. That energy created a lot of trouble for people who make decisions for others that they would never think about doing themselves. That energy will get people killed or locked up for the rest of their lives, or they will walk around the community like they did not do anything wrong, because the community will accept that energy before they accept an energy that is at peace with itself. This is because they have the same sick lifestyles that the peaceful energy does not have. That misguided energy will manifest in drinking, some are on drugs, and will create some fake heart and try to do something that they know will get them knocked down. But they get back up and do it over and over again until they find somebody to kill them. That is what you call dangerous energy. It is out of control, and you have to walk lightly around them, because they have a death wish and want to destroy lives with them.

I truly believe that people should get a second and third and fourth chance, because I feel that the government plays a big part in changing the direction the country is going. They are setting traps for the people to destroy their lives. One, they broke down the school system just so they could to have blue collar workers do our work in the communities. Some people like doing that work with a college education, but they choose to do that on their own. Others are forced because the school system failed them. Two, the government put liquor stores and drug strips all through communities where people are in a stressed environment. Three, the government allowed all kinds of sexual lifestyles in the communities, confusing the kids when they are young and impressionable. Then they grow up with those lifestyles and then become out of control. Four, the government lets all kinds of bad food into the communities without regulating them. That messes with your body and mind over a period of time. And five, TV plays a big part with all of these violent shows, glorifying them, and people start imitating it as a way of life. Then the government makes some people think that that's the way of their culture is supposed to be. See, our government pushed all these toxins into the communities, and it seems like a person has to do wrong before they notice that something is not right. Then the government comes along and locks that person up for the rest of their life for something that was out of their control.

And I also watch how people take materialistic things and try to make it energy. You will see some people so caught up with their clothes that nothing else matters. I've watched people that have nothing — no job, no place to stay, no money to feed themselves — but will walk down that street like they run the country, wearing a slick outfit, shoes shined, clothes coordinated, and so proud of the outfit they have on that it plays tricks with their mind, fooling themselves into thinking that they are all right. Or, you will see a person take a car and put so much money into it that it seems like the car is the only thing they care about. People are so caught up in the materialistic world that the real energy that flows around them is unrecognizable — they do not recognize what they have around them. See, the materialistic world took the place of the natural things to throw us off balance so we would not understand our inherent nature that keeps us balanced. I witness people dying from drinking and drugs who might have a donor organ inside them, but the forces of wrong that they are used to will run them back into a world where they know what is not good for them. I could not understand what would make a person want to hurt themselves so badly. The only conclusion that I came up with is that when I was like that, I wanted to stop messing with drugs, but I was too weak to stop. Going to jail helped me a lot because I did not have the strength to do it myself.

I also believe that legalizing natural drugs for medical use is a good thing, because I never heard about a person's liver of kidneys getting damaged from natural drugs like they do from artificial drugs. I also feel that the government is locking people up and giving them too much time for drug charges with no violence, because I feel that it's only right for a person to choose the high they prefer for themselves. Alcohol and cigarettes do more damage to the organs in the body than the other natural drugs. It's the chemicals in the drugs they use to process these drugs that are causing them to do harm, not the natural drugs. I think the government is using double standards by making some drugs illegal and some legal. And if the government approves natural drugs, I think the water systems will be better for drinking the water that is processed by them, because fewer chemicals will have to be used to try to filter out the system. It will also help the living creatures that live in the water.

I do not believe that those programs really help people to get off of their codependency, because they depend on other legal drugs to help them, or going to meetings for the rest of their lives. Life programs them to think that they cannot think without a counselor telling them what's right or wrong.

Once you lose your energy, you are the only one who can find it. You have to be strong enough to block out all the wrong forces that are trying to control your life — like the fake world that gets so much publicity for doing nothing but acting. We are programmed to think that the artificial things are more important than the real world. See, we're not happy just living and having a normal job, because TV has programmed us to think that life is too hard. But it fails to say that they put thoughts into the country's citizens' minds that make us act that way. All you have to do is look at when it's time for an election. We will see all kinds of candidates telling the people everything they think you want to hear, hoping that they are speaking the truth. But in the end we go back to reality, knowing that it was just an election and nothing else. Then to top it off, we have all kinds of lifestyles in the communities that are confusing the young kids. The government allows them in the communities just to confuse the kids and to support the big businesses in the country.

Have you ever wondered want happened to the mad scientists that they used to talk about in the olden days? What happened was they were incorporated into these big companies. Because you know that they still exist in the world today, but maybe they are not recognized as being mad anymore, because being in a civilized society it's legal to create things that are not right for the world. Are they being protected by some kind of law that says that as long as something gets approved by the FDA and other inspection agencies, it's all right for their crazy thinking to exist in the world today? And I also wonder, why do the government officials get on TV and talk about something that is illegal, but allow organizations that support their cause to cover up every wrong they do to the communities? And what makes a person run for office and talk about taking a stand against corrupted companies that are poisoning the communities, giving all the control that they need, and then turning around and abusing it? Why does that happen over and over again? Is something wrong with that particular person, or is something wrong with America to allow that to exist among our high officials that run the country?

I really think that the people are waiting for the church to take a stand, to do something, and when that day comes, you will see all kinds of people standing beside them — once the church takes a stand against the hypocritical preachers and brings them to religious court for changing the rules. They do not have enough strength within them to follow the old rules, and that is why they made religion turn the way it is today. They say you can make a new religion and call it what you want, but you cannot take an old religion and change it. That's illegal. You remember that song they used to sing in the olden days, "Give me that old time religion, and give me that old time religion because it's good enough for me"? So if you take the old time religion and change it, then it's not old anymore, then we should not be talking about the faith that the old religion brought us. We cannot have both, because they do not belong together. I believe that there's nothing wrong with restriction, because nature restricts us every day — from eating too much, from doing too much of anything. Your body has to rest, and then you can start the process all over again.

I hope that the younger kids understand what I am saying because their strength is there, and they can make a big difference in changing the world when their time comes. Keep your strength and stay grounded, because you will experience a lot of wrong things that will come to challenge you and try to throw you off your square. You have to be able to accept the challenge and beat it and learn from it in order to leave a legacy of how to fight the dead energy that is placed around you as a trap so you can fall victim to the wrong ways. Then close the door to leave it well off for the next one that comes behind you. And if you fail, I do not know the words to describe what they have in store for this country, but I can say travel to the past and open your eyes, and you will see the future. It might be too late for your parents, but it's never too late for the young.

Thanks for taking the time to read my parable. May peace and blessings be with you at all times?

—Heyward C. Sanders